A New Friend?

I thought Ginger looked a little uneasy as we listened to Kate and Stephanie and Patti come running up the stairs. I couldn't really blame her. After all, she was about to meet three more new people.

Stephanie was the first to burst through the door. Ginger held out her hand, but before Stephanie could shake it, Kate came rushing into the room. "Virginia?" she announced. "I'm Kate Beekman."

"Ginger," I mumbled.

But Kate was running on: "Listen, Lauren, I have to turn on the TV for a minute. . . ."

Meanwhile, Stephanie started checking out her hair in the mirror. "Why is it that as soon as it gets the teeniest bit damp outside," she wailed, "my head looks like it belongs on the bride of Frankenstein?!"

Ginger looked a little lost, but fortunately at that moment Patti spoke to her. "Hi, Ginger—I'm Patti Jenkins. When did you get to Riverhurst?" Good old Patti. At least *she* could be counted on to make polite conversation. It was getting to the point where I was more worried that Ginger wouldn't like Kate and Stephanie, than the other way around.

Look for these and other books
in the Sleepover Friends Series:

SLEEPOVER FRIENDS

Lauren in the Middle

Susan Saunders

AN
APPLE
PAPERBACK

SCHOLASTIC INC.
New York Toronto London Auckland Sydney

ISBN 0-590-42816-0

12 11 10 9 8 7 6 5 4 3 2 1   0 1 2 3 4 5/9

Printed in the U.S.A.   28

First Scholastic printing, January 1990

Lauren in the Middle

Chapter
1

"Lauren!" my dad called from downstairs. "They're here!"

"Coming!" I yelled back. I ran a comb through my hair, which was looking even stragglier than it usually does. There's not all that much you can do with medium-brown hair that's fine and as straight as a stick — especially when the weather's been nothing but rain, sleet, and snow for weeks on end.

A second later our doorbell rang, and I heard people talking in the front hall.

"George!" Mr. Blaney boomed out. George is my dad, and Mr. Blaney's my dad's boss at Blaney Real Estate. "And Marion! I'd like you to meet my niece, Virginia — Virginia Kinkaid." Mr. Blaney paused for a breath. "Honey, this is Mr. and Mrs. Hunter."

"Nice to meet you both," a girl's voice said. It was a slow, kind of husky voice, with a little bit of a Southern accent on the *i*'s — "Nahs to meet you. . . ." She went on, "But nearly everybody calls me Ginger."

Ginger Kinkaid — what a great name! I liked the way she sounded, too. Maybe things were finally looking up after months of winter gloomies. I grinned and pitched the comb onto my bed, just missing my kitten, Rocky. Then I dashed out of my bedroom.

"Lauren!" my dad called again.

But I was already halfway there.

"And here's Lauren!" Mr. Blaney announced from the bottom of the stairs. He's a tall man, sort of egg-shaped, with bristly reddish-brown hair and eyebrows to match. "Lauren, this is Ginger."

Ginger had reddish-brown hair, too, but there was nothing bristly about it. It was long, thick, and wavy, and she'd coiled it up on the sides so you could see her earrings: tiny gold scallop shells. Ginger isn't pretty, exactly, but she's definitely interesting looking. She's a little shorter than me and has big brown eyes, a narrow nose, and pale peach skin. That day she was wearing a yellow-and-green argyle sweater, black jeans, and yellow canvas sneakers.

She was also wearing a big smile. "Hey, Lauren," she said, sticking out her hand. "It's awfully nahs of you to have me sleep over."

Most fifth-graders I know don't shake hands, and it made me feel pretty grown-up to shake hers. "Hi, Ginger," I said. "I'm glad you could come." I actually meant it, even though it had been my dad's idea, and Mr. Blaney had asked *him*.

Mr. Blaney rocked back on his heels enthusiastically and beamed at Ginger and me. "I know you two are going to be great pals!" he said. Then he handed over a big blue tote. "Here are Virginia's — er — Ginger's overnight things."

"Thank you, Uncle Bud," Ginger said, giving him a kiss on the cheek. "See you tomorrow."

"My room is upstairs," I told Ginger, starting back up the steps with the tote. "Good night, Mr. Blaney."

"Good night, girls," Mr. Blaney said. "Have fun!"

"Isn't he a sweet old thing?" Ginger murmured as soon as we'd turned the corner. "He'd do *anything* for me. He thought this would be a good way for me to meet a few people before I start school on Monday. But Uncle Bud is awfully old-fashioned. I let everyone know I didn't want to be 'Virginia' as soon as I could *talk!*"

I was impressed. Here's somebody who knew her own mind when she was *two*, I thought to myself. And I'm almost eleven, and I still don't know mine half the time. Out loud to Ginger I said, "My dad told me you're from North Carolina."

"Um-hmm. And Florida before that, and Illinois for a while," Ginger replied. "We traveled a lot while my dad was a captain in the Air Force."

That sounded kind of exciting to me. I've lived in Riverhurst my whole life. "And now he'll be working at Blaney Real Estate?" I asked as I led her down the hall toward my bedroom.

Ginger nodded. "I think Riverhurst is it for a good, long while," she said. "Daddy's really looking forward to working with Uncle Bud."

My father said that Ginger's dad would be setting up a whole new computer system. It would hook Blaney up with other real estate companies all across the United States, which sounded kind of neat. I love fooling around with computers myself.

"Daddy designed all these computer programs for the Air Force," Ginger went on. "He's sort of a mathematical genius."

"I'm no genius, but I'm a lot better at math than I am at English or History," I admitted.

"Me, too!" Ginger said. "I bet we have lots of stuff in common, Lauren. Like what's your favorite color?"

I looked down at my blue sweater with white squiggles. "Blue," I said.

"Wow — that's amazing!" said Ginger. "Mine is, too." She followed me through the door of my bedroom. "Great room!"

"Thanks," I said. My room isn't *really* all that special: I've got bunk beds, a desk, a chest of drawers, and a couple of bookshelves. That night it was neater than usual, though — I'd cleaned up especially for the sleepover.

"You're sure neater than I am," Ginger went on, as if she were reading my mind. "My mom's always talking about how she needs a bulldozer to shovel out *my* junk!" I couldn't help grinning. Ginger Kinkaid and I were definitely on the same wavelength!

"And that's a fabulous poster!" She pointed to a shot of Kevin DeSpain in pleated jeans and a leather bomber jacket. Kevin's on *Made for Each Other* on Tuesday nights, with Marcy Monroe. He's the super-cute guy with dark wavy hair and big green eyes.

5

"He's my all-time favorite actor!" she added.

"Mine, too," I said. "Wasn't he great in *Too Soon to Love* with Tanya Colter?"

"Dynamite!" Ginger said.

"Kate sure didn't think so," I said, more to myself than to Ginger. That was an understatement. Kate claimed Kevin DeSpain deserved to win The Worst Actor of All Time Award for his performance in *Too Soon to Love*. It was actually kind of nice to have someone agree with me about movies for a change. . . .

"Who's Kate?" Ginger asked, sitting down on the bottom bunk.

"Kate Beekman, one of the girls who's sleeping over tonight," I replied. "She lives just one house down. Kate's a real movie freak — new, old, black-and-white, color, horror movies, musicals. You name it, she'll watch it. She wants to be a movie director some day. And when it comes to movies she has very strong opinions," I added.

Ginger looked thoughtful. "Who else is coming over?" she asked.

"My friend Stephanie Green," I said. "She grew up in the city. She's really outgoing, and she knows lots about fashion. By *fourth grade*, she already had her own look. She almost always wears a combination of red, black, and white."

"Red, black, and white?" Ginger said doubtfully. "Day in and day out? Doesn't that get a little boring?"

I'd never thought of it that way before. "Well, not really," I said. "Stephanie has curly black hair, so she looks great in red, black, and white. Anyway, she says limiting her colors lets her focus on the styles. And the third person you'll meet tonight," I went on, "is Patti Jenkins. She's just about the nicest person I know, and she's really smart, too."

"So which one is your best friend," Ginger asked.

"Best friend?" I repeated. "We're all best friends."

"You can't have three *best* friends," Ginger said firmly. "There must be one you like a little more than the others."

I shook my head. "Not in our gang," I said. It was true. In our gang, it was one for all and all for one, even though I *have* known Kate years longer than Stephanie or Patti.

Kate and I are practically next-door neighbors on Pine Street, so we just naturally started playing together before we were even out of diapers. By kindergarten, we were seeing each other almost every day. That's when the sleepovers started. Every Friday night, either Kate would sleep over at my house, or I would sleep over at hers. Kate's dad named us The Sleepover Twins, but we couldn't have been less alike. Kate's short and blonde; I'm tall and dark. She's super neat; I'm messy to the max. Kate's sensible; I've been known to let my imagination run away with me. Still, as different as we are, it was always Kate and me, first, last, and always.

In the early days we played endless games of Grown-ups and Let's Pretend. But by second grade, we'd graduated to Truth or Dare and Mad Libs, not to mention watching every movie we could find on Friday-night TV, some of them two and three times.

Even though we spent thousands of hours together, it wasn't until last year that Kate and I ever had a really major disagreement. That's when Stephanie Green moved to Riverhurst from the city. She and I got to know each other because we were both in 4A, Mr. Civello's class.

I thought Stephanie was great. She had all these stories about life in the city, and she had neat ideas about clothes and hair styles. I wanted Kate to get to know her, too, so I invited Stephanie to a Friday night sleepover at my house.

It was a total disaster! Kate thought Stephanie was a stuck-up airhead who only talked about shopping. Stephanie thought Kate was a stuffy know-it-all. It didn't look good for a lasting friendship or even a second meeting.

But I can be pretty stubborn when I want to be. Since all three of us live on Pine Street, I got Stephanie to start riding her bike to school and back with Kate and me. One day Stephanie invited Kate and me to spend a Friday night at her house. And little by little, the Sleepover Twins grew into a threesome.

Not that Kate and Stephanie suddenly saw eye to eye on everything. No way! That's just one of the reasons I was glad when Patti Jenkins turned up in Mrs. Mead's class this fall, along with the rest of us. Patti's from the city, too, although you'd never know it to talk to her. She's as quiet and shy as Stephanie is outgoing.

Patti's kind, and thoughtful, and she's great at smoothing things over when people get prickly. Stephanie wanted Patti to be part of our gang, and Kate and I both liked her right away. So it wasn't long before there were *four* Sleepover Friends!

I looked over at Ginger Kinkaid, sitting on my bed and petting Rocky. Was it possible there were soon to be *five* Sleepover Friends?!

Ginger was friendly and fun. She had great hair, she was a neat dresser, she had a terrific accent, and so far she and I seemed to be in total agreement about *everything*. "What's not to like?" I said to myself. But I wondered what everybody else was going to think of her. Especially Kate, who's usually the most particular.

"I've known Kate the longest," I said to Ginger. "So I guess I would say she's my *best* best friend. . . ."

"Lauren?" Kate herself yelled from downstairs.

"We're on our way up!" Patti and Stephanie called out together.

10

Chapter
2

I thought Ginger looked a little uneasy as we listened to Kate and Stephanie and Patti come running up the stairs. I couldn't really blame her. After all, she was about to meet three more new people, and she'd hardly had time to get comfortable with me.

Stephanie was the first to burst through the door. She was wearing her red down jacket, with her mom's rhinestone lightning bolt pinned to the collar. "Hi!" she said. "You must be Virginia!"

"Ginger," I corrected her. "Ginger Kinkaid meet Stephanie Green."

Ginger held out her hand, but before Stephanie could shake it, Kate came rushing into the room. "Virginia?" she announced. "I'm Kate Beekman."

11

"Ginger," I mumbled.

But Kate was running on, "Listen, Lauren, I have to turn on the TV for a minute. . . ." Kate's spent practically as much time in my house as I have, so she doesn't stand on ceremony. "I've been watching *Lion of the Desert*, this great, old silent movie on Channel 24, and I don't want to miss the end!"

Without waiting for an answer, Kate dumped her backpack on the floor, and switched on my parents' portable, which I'd borrowed for the evening. Old friends can act that way with each other, but I hoped Ginger wasn't thinking that Kate was a little bossy.

Meanwhile, Stephanie pulled off her jacket and started checking out her hair in the mirror on the back of my closet door. "Why is it that as soon as it gets the teeniest bit damp outside," she wailed, "my head looks like it belongs on the bride of Frankenstein?!" Stephanie gets totally distracted by the frizzies.

Ginger looked a little lost, but fortunately at that moment Patti spoke to her. "Hi, Ginger — I'm Patti Jenkins," she said in her soft voice. She sat down on my desk chair and leaned forward encouragingly. "When did you get to Riverhurst?"

I breathed a sigh of relief. Good old Patti. At

12

least *she* could be counted on to make polite conversation. It was getting to the point where I was more worried that Ginger wouldn't like Kate and Stephanie, than the other way around.

"Just this afternoon," Ginger said. "The moving van won't be here with our stuff until tomorrow, though."

"What street is your house on?" Stephanie asked. She'd stopped trying to mash her curls flat. She was leaning against my desk, sizing up Ginger.

"Deerfield Lane," Ginger said.

Kate was practically glued to the TV set, where guys in flowing robes were racing their horses silently across the screen. Kate's a little nearsighted, but she hates to wear her glasses, so when she's watching TV she sits just about on top of it. But she managed to murmur over the silent-movie music, "Deerfield. Isn't that where Christy Soames lives, Stephanie?"

Christy Soames is this real snob in Mr. Patterson's room who latched on to Stephanie for a while. All she cares about is clothes designers and labels. Stephanie loves to shop, but Christy was too much even for her.

"Who's she?" Ginger asked.

"A girl in 5C," I answered. "The four of us are all in 5B, Mrs. Mead's class."

The movie music got louder, with lots of long drum rolls. A man in a white cape swept a woman onto his black horse and galloped away across the desert. Then the music faded, and a big, black-and-white "The End" appeared in the middle of the screen.

"That was excellent!" was Kate's verdict. She switched off the set. "Ramon Seville was fantastic. No wonder he was the biggest star in Hollywood when he made *Lion of the Desert*!"

"Give me Kevin DeSpain any time," Ginger declared, with a knowing glance in my direction. "Nobody's ever been better than Kevin in *Sands of the Sahara*."

"Kevin DeSpain?" Kate said indignantly. "He's not an actor at all! He's a . . . a . . . TV personality! Like Spunky, the Wonder Dog!"

Ginger shrugged. "All I know is, he's the best. Right, Lauren?" She grinned at me, and I grinned back. As I said, it was kind of nice to have somebody agree with me about movies for a change.

But Kate's used to having the last word, *especially* about films, and she didn't like it one bit. When I noticed the scowl on her face I decided to change the subject fast. "Let's go load up on some grub," I said brightly. "I'm starting to get hungry."

14

"So what else is new?" Stephanie teased. "We call Lauren the Endless Stomach," she explained to Ginger. "She has to feed it constantly, or it turns mean."

"I'm feeling kind of hungry myself," Ginger said. "And even if Lauren does eat a lot, it sure doesn't show." I am skinny. Luckily for me, I'm like my mom and Roger. No matter how much I scarf down, I stay thin.

"It's very depressing," Stephanie went on. "Lauren can gobble up everything in sight, but if I eat one tiny piece of candy, two seconds later my face is fatter!" She pinched her cheeks, which *are* a little rounder than mine. "But I can always diet tomorrow," she added. "Lead me to the food!"

The five of us clattered down the stairs to the kitchen, where Kate, Stephanie, Patti, and I got busy gathering together the munchies. Patti opened the cabinet next to the sink and took out some plates. Meanwhile, Stephanie dropped ice cubes into five glasses and started pouring the Dr Pepper. Kate rummaged around in the refrigerator, while I opened a king-size bag of nacho-flavored chips and dumped them into a big plastic bowl.

The four of us have gone through the sleepover-snacks routine so often that we're like an assembly line. The only problem was that it didn't leave anything for Ginger to do. But then she spotted a box of my mom's bridge cards, left out on the kitchen counter.

Ginger shook the cards out of their box. She hunted through them until she found the queen of spades, laid it on the kitchen table, face up, and shuffled the deck. I watched as she dealt another card on top of the queen, also face up. Then she put a third card down to the right of the first two, a fourth card above them, and another below. . . .

"What kind of weird card game is that?" Stephanie asked, setting down the Dr Pepper bottle.

Ginger glanced up to find all four of us staring at her. She quickly scooped the cards up and shook her head, looking embarrassed. "Oh, nothing, really," she mumbled. "I was just laying out the cards to tell Lauren's fortune."

"Oh, no!" Kate groaned. "You don't believe in that mumbo-jumbo, too? Lauren, did you put her up to this?"

I shot her a can't-you-be-more-polite look while Stephanie giggled. I should have expected it. If there's one thing that gets Kate crazy, it's what she calls "mumbo-jumbo," which includes just about everything from fortune-tellers and horoscopes to flying saucers and alien visitors.

I don't happen to agree, which is another reason Kate is always accusing me of having a runaway imagination. And I guess Ginger didn't, either. Her cheeks got kind of pink. And she looked Kate straight in the eye. "Oh, reeeeally?" she drawled. "If it's such mumbo-jumbo, then why have people believed in it for thousands — "

Hoping to block a Beekman explosion, I interrupted: "Why don't you show us how it works upstairs?" I grabbed one tray piled with plates and drinks and food. Patti picked up the second tray, and we hustled out of the kitchen.

When we got to my room, we put the trays down on the rug. While Kate and Stephanie uncovered the containers from the fridge, Patti and I watched Ginger deal the cards onto my desk.

"The queen of clubs and the queen of spades are for dark-haired girls," Ginger said to us in her husky voice. "The queen of hearts and the queen of diamonds are for blondes."

She set the queen of spades down again. Then she started dealing cards on top of and around the queen.

"Come on, guys — park it!" Kate ordered from her place on the rug.

"Yeah, aren't you going to eat?" Stephanie added, skimming a chip across the top of my special onion-soup dip. "I thought you guys were hungry."

"Give us a second," I murmured.

"Usually, I'd deal ten cards, but this time I'll stop with five," Ginger told Patti and me.

"What do they mean?" Patti asked, studying the cards on the table. For a person who's a whiz at science, she's a lot more open-minded about "mumbo-jumbo" than Kate, or Stephanie.

"The card on top of the queen stands for the most important thing that's happening to Lauren right now," Ginger said, pointing to a jack of clubs. "A Jack means a young person, and clubs mean hobbies, or friends. . . ."

"My hobby right now is jogging with Roger," I said. "And Roger's already seventeen."

"But Ginger's younger," Patti pointed out.

"And *she's* a new friend!" I said excitedly.

"I suppose the Jack *could* stand for me," Ginger said thoughtfully.

Kate groaned impatiently. Patti, Ginger, and I ignored her, and leaned closer to the cards.

"The card on the right," Ginger went on, tapping the four of spades, "represents a problem you may have in the future. The number four has to do with health. . . ."

"I have a dentist appointment in two weeks," I volunteered. "Wow, I hope this doesn't mean I'll have lots of cavities!" I added gloomily.

"It probably means you'll have a hangnail," Kate said, with a giggle.

Ginger moved on to the seven of diamonds at the top. "This card stands for a goal you'll be trying to reach," she said. "Seven means success and diamonds mean business, or money."

"Success in business could be the raffle!" Patti exclaimed.

"Really, Patti!" Kate sputtered, putting down the chicken leg she was holding.

"What raffle?" Ginger asked me, wrinkling her nose at Kate. Something told me the two of them weren't exactly hitting it off. . . . On the other hand, Kate and Stephanie hadn't taken to each other at first, either.

"It's a raffle to raise money for supplies for the new art studio at school," I explained. "The winner gets an all-expenses-paid trip for two to San Francisco."

"And whoever sells the most tickets to the raffle

19

gets a prize, too," Patti said. "If the winner's a girl she'll get this fabulous, embroidered jacket from Just Juniors. Just Juniors is a really great store at the mall," she added for Ginger's benefit.

Everybody at Riverhurst Elementary had started out with ten raffle tickets each, but all four of us were already on our second ten. Actually, Stephanie was on her *third*. Stephanie's a great salesperson. She can talk almost anyone into almost anything. She'd already sold tickets to all of her neighbors, even the Williamses, who have their *own* kid at Riverhurst Elementary to buy from! Plus Stephanie's dad's a lawyer at Blake, Binder, and Rosten, and he'd sold tickets to Mr. Blake, Mr. Binder, and Mr. Rosten, and to some of her father's clients, too.

"If one of us gets the jacket," Stephanie went on, "we plan to share it among the four of us! It's fantastic. We all tried it on at Just Juniors last weekend."

"We'll know next Friday," Patti said. "That's the day of the drawing."

"Lauren," Kate broke in crossly, "your dip's going to turn to concrete!"

"I guess we better eat," Ginger said stiffly.

So she, Patti, and I sat down on the rug next to

Kate and Stephanie and started digging in.

"Where did you learn to do that?" Stephanie asked Ginger, pointing to the cards spread out on my desk.

"At a summer camp I go to," Ginger replied. She snared a chicken wing and served herself a heaping spoonful of my special dip. "It's called Camp Minnewaska."

"Oh. Yeah," Stephanie said. "I've heard of that place — it's in Pennsylvania."

The snacks seemed to calm everybody down. When we'd each had a couple of helpings of cold chicken, chips, and dip, Ginger made us a fabulous banana-peanut-butter-chocolate shake in the kitchen in mom's blender. With those ingredients it had to be yummy, and it was!

We headed back upstairs to watch TV with our glasses refilled to the brim. Ginger gathered up the cards. She paused for a moment, though, and laid the queen of diamonds face up on the desktop.

Queen of diamonds means a blonde girl, I said to myself. Only Stephanie said it out loud.

"Hey, that's you, Kate," she announced, taking a long sip of Ginger's shake. She must have been paying closer attention than I'd thought when Ginger

21

ran through the meanings of the cards the first time.

On top of the queen, Ginger placed an eight of clubs.

"Clubs — friends or hobbies?" Patti said.

Ginger nodded.

"But what does the eight mean?" I asked her.

"Trouble!" Ginger said, loud enough for Kate to have heard in the next *county*. "Trouble with friends for a blonde girl!"

Kate put down her milkshake. "This is one dumb game!" she growled. "For a change of pace, why don't we do something *fun*?!"

She glared at Ginger, and Ginger glared back. But then Stephanie said brightly, "I have an idea! What about a nice, friendly game of Truth or Dare?"

Chapter
3

Truth or Dare is a great game for close friends to play, because you learn things about each other that you'd probably never know otherwise. That's how we found out that Kate's most embarrassing moment was wetting her pants when she fell off the seesaw in first grade. Or that Patti had secretly thought for months that Donald Foster — who lives between Kate and me — was the cutest boy in Riverhurst.

But when you play Truth or Dare with people you haven't met before, or with people who might not like each other much, then you're *really* dealing with the unknown. That makes the game a lot more exciting — maybe too exciting. After all, Kate and

Ginger were *already* rubbing each other the wrong way!

The game started out smoothly enough. Since Stephanie had suggested that we play in the first place, she got to choose the first victim. "Lauren," she said sweetly, "truth or dare?"

I had to give it serious thought. Would I feel funnier answering an embarrassing question in front of an almost total stranger? Or would a dare be even more gruesome?

Remembering some of the dares Stephanie's come up with in the past — like making me invite the biggest nerd in school to the movies — I decided I'd better stay far away from them! "Um . . . truth," I said. I gritted my teeth, expecting the worst.

But I guess Stephanie didn't want things to get any more shaky than they were already. "If you were shipwrecked on a desert island," she said, "which boy at Riverhurst Elementary would you most want to have shipwrecked with you?"

I grinned at Stephanie gratefully. Not only was the question not embarrassing, it was actually fun to think about. The point would be to get rescued, right? So, who would be most likely to do that?

None of the sixth-graders, I decided. They were

all too full of themselves to think up anything useful. What about Pete Stone? Pete's a boy in our class. He and I were sort of interested in each other at the beginning of the year, but that's ancient history.

I shook my head. Judging from the way Pete acts with girls — hanging around with one girl, only to drop her and start up with another one — he wouldn't be very dependable. Mark Freedman? Nope. He'd be too happy playing baseball with any coconuts he found lying around. Henry Larkin? Henry's cute, and funny, but he's much too lazy to build a raft. Besides, Henry would think being shipwrecked was great — just like a permanent vacation.

I was busy running through the rest of the fifth-grade boys in my head when the perfect answer hit me. "Walter Williams!" I said.

"Walter Williams?!" Stephanie shrieked.

"You have to be kidding, Lauren," Kate said. Patti started to giggle.

Walter Williams lives in the house behind Stephanie's — his parents are the ones who bought a raffle ticket from her. He's only eight-and-a-half, and I'm at least a foot taller than he is, but Walter just happens to have an IQ that goes right through the roof!

"Walter is very intelligent, but he's only in the

fourth grade," Patti explained to Ginger. She and Walter are both in the Quarks Club, for kids who are super-smart in science.

"Highly romantic, Lauren," Stephanie said, snickering at the very idea.

"Who'd be more likely to get me rescued?" I replied. "Walter Williams or Taylor Sprouse?"

Taylor's one of those sixth-graders I mentioned. He plays not-very-good guitar, dresses all in black like Russell Carter, the lead singer of the Boodles, and checks himself out in every mirror or plate-glass window he passes.

"You've got a point there," Stephanie admitted. "Walter Williams, natch."

Now it was my turn to choose someone for Truth or Dare. I glanced around the circle, trying to make up my mind who to pick. I knew no one would make Patti do or say anything too awful, because she's too nice to take advantage of. So she didn't need my help. That left Ginger and Kate. . . .

I decided I'd have to count on Kate being careful with Ginger, who was *company* after all. Ginger, on the other hand, seemed to be getting more and more irritated with Kate every second. I noticed that every time she even glanced in Kate's direction, she had this way of chewing on her bottom lip. I was sure if

I picked Ginger, she'd call on Kate next, and who knew what might happen then?

I decided I'd better choose Kate. "Truth or dare?" I asked her.

"Truth," Kate said. Obviously, she'd made up her mind not to take any chances with dares, either.

"Tell us one major thing you've been keeping a secret," I said. I was being easy on her. Kate keeps lots of secrets. Usually we don't hear about them until they're not even worth knowing — so she'd have a wide choice.

"Okay," Kate said briskly. "I don't like Royce Mason anymore." Royce is a seventh-grader. He has curly brown hair and brown eyes, and he plays on the junior-high soccer team. Kate's had a crush on him for ages!

"What?!" I squawked. After all, I'm Kate's *best* best friend, and she hadn't even hinted about it to me!

"When did that happen?" Stephanie wanted to know. "And why?"

"And who *do* you like now?" Patti asked.

"No more information," Kate said smugly. "I've answered the question. Now it's my turn."

She swiveled around a little on the rug and looked straight at Ginger Kinkaid. Uh-oh, I thought.

27

"Ginger, truth . . . or dare?" Kate said softly.

Ginger's eyes met mine for a split-second. Then she turned her head and stared right back at Kate. "Dare!" she said coolly.

"Fine!" Kate said. "Go outdoors. Walk around Donald Foster's house to the far side, tap on the third window from the end — that's Donald's room — and introduce yourself. Oh, and you have to bring *proof* that you actually talked to him."

"Kate!" Even Stephanie looked surprised. "Ginger doesn't know where Donald Foster lives. She doesn't know who Donald Foster *is*!"

"Well, it's not too hard to show her his house," Kate said huffily. "It's right next door. She can't miss it!"

"But it's sleeting!" I protested.

"It's stopped," Kate said, pointing out my bedroom window.

"What about Lauren's parents?" Patti asked. "If they see us outside at eleven fifteen at night. . . ."

"I'll bet they're already asleep by now." Kate seemed to have all the answers. I sighed. She was really set on embarrassing Ginger with this dare of hers.

I scrambled to my feet and pushed open my door a crack. I peered down the hall at my parents' bed-

28

room door. There wasn't any light shining under it. "They *are* asleep," I admitted. "But you don't have to do it, Ginger."

But Ginger had already stood up. She picked up her jacket from the end of my bed. "No problem," she said. "Let's go."

The four of us tiptoed down the stairs behind her. When we got to the bottom, I tried to talk her out of it again. "I'm sure Kate would let you off the hook," I said, even though Kate didn't say a word to back me up.

But Ginger replied: "I chose *dare*, didn't I?" Then she marched across the kitchen to the back door. I could tell there was no way she'd ever back down in front of Kate Beekman.

Roger was out on a date with his girlfriend, Linda, so we didn't have to worry about him catching us. And our dog, Bullwinkle, was sleeping in the garage that night, so he couldn't sound an alarm, either.

I unlocked the door, and all five of us crept out onto the back porch.

"Brrr!" Stephanie said, shivering. "It's cold out here! We should have brought our jackets."

"I'm freezing," Kate agreed. "Anyway, the Fosters' house is right there. Say 'hi' to Donald for me," she added. Then she and Stephanie hurried back into the kitchen.

That left Ginger and Patti and me huddled on the cold porch.

"You'll have to crawl through the hedge," I told Ginger, "cross their backyard, and tap on his window." I stopped and shuffled my feet. "Actually, Ginger," I said in a lower voice, "you could just *say* you tapped it, and nobody came."

"No way," Ginger said, shaking her head firmly. "I'm going to talk to Donald Foster, in person, and bring back proof I did it. You can bet on that!"

"Okay, okay," I said. "Just so you'll be prepared — Donald's a seventh-grader, and he's incredibly conceited."

"I think he's perfectly nice," Patti said softly. "And awfully cute," she murmured. I rolled my eyes and sighed. Not only does *Patti* think Donald Foster is the cutest boy in Riverhurst, so does Stephanie, and at least half the other girls in town under the age of fourteen. But, most importantly, so does Donald Foster. He's definitely his own biggest fan.

"We'll wait just inside the door for you," I went on. I should have waited for Ginger outside, but my teeth were beginning to chatter.

As soon as Ginger reached the hedge between

30

my house and the Fosters', Patti and I dashed back into the warm kitchen. Kate and Stephanie were slouched around the table, waiting.

"Really, Kate!" I said. "That's kind of a hard dare, for somebody who's never even been in Riverhurst before! Wandering around in the dark in a strange place, having to deal with Donald Foster. . . ." I was starting to get mad just thinking about it. Besides, I suddenly realized that if Ginger told Mr. Blaney about it, I could get into serious trouble with my dad! "Why are you being so tough on her, Kate?"

Kate shifted in her chair. "I don't like her attitude!" she said. She tightened her lips into a thin, straight line.

"What's wrong with her attitude?" I said. "You're the one who gripes and moans practically every time she opens her mouth!"

Kate looked a little guilty. "What about all that fortune-telling garbage?" she muttered. "And threatening me with *trouble* with friends?!"

"Guys, guys!" Stephanie said, holding up her hands for quiet. "You're giving me a headache!"

Kate and I frowned at each other. We hadn't been this close to a fight since Stephanie first moved to Riverhurst.

"Don't you think Ginger should be back by

now?'' Patti asked in the silence that followed. ''It's been almost ten minutes.''

Ten minutes? I gulped. It shouldn't take more than five, tops, to crawl through the hedge, dash across the Fosters' yard, tap on Donald's window, say a few words, and dash back with his name scrawled on a piece of paper, or something! I hurried to the door and looked out. Patti was right behind me.

''I don't see her,'' I said, squinting toward the hedge.

Kate and Stephanie shoved their chairs back and joined us.

But there was no sign of Ginger Kinkaid anywhere.

''She's probably on the other side of the bushes still trying to get up her nerve,'' Kate said smugly.

''I don't think so,'' I said sharply. There was nothing wrong with Ginger's nerve, as far as I could tell.

''What if she's stepped in a hole and twisted her ankle?'' Stephanie said.

''This could be a major catastrophe!'' I said grimly. ''My dad's boss isn't going to be too happy if his favorite niece disappears during my sleepover! I'm going to go look for her.''

"Me, too," Patti said.

As we raced upstairs for our jackets, Stephanie hissed after us, "Bring ours down, too!"

The four of us were just zipping them up when Ginger Kinkaid finally appeared on the back porch.

I ran to the door and let her in. "What happened?" I said.

"Are you okay?" Patti asked. Ginger seemed fine — her cheeks were a little red, that was all.

"And where did you get that cap?" Stephanie said.

Ginger was wearing a green knitted cap with "Riverhurst Tigers" printed in white across the front.

"Oh, this?" Ginger took the cap off and glanced at it casually. "Donald and I had a nice, long talk," she drawled, sneaking a quick look at Kate. "And then he gave his cap to me, as proof that I'd met him. And you were right, Patti — he *is* a perfectly nice boy."

And Ginger handed her Donald Foster's cap.

33

Chapter
4

Our game of Truth or Dare broke up after that. Kate said she was really tired. She also said that since she didn't think there was enough space in my room for all *five* people to sleep comfortably, she would sleep in the spare bedroom. Stephanie went in there with her.

I gave Ginger and Patti the bunks in my room, and I rolled up in a sleeping bag on the floor.

I didn't fall asleep right away, though. This was the first time Kate, Patti, Stephanie, and I had split up during a sleepover, and I felt very uneasy about it. I lay there on the rug, tossing and turning for what seemed like hours! Finally I managed to doze off. I had a horrible dream. It was about the end of the Sleepover Friends.

Kate and Stephanie had taken Patti and me to court to make us stop calling ourselves the Sleepover Friends. Mr. Green was their lawyer. "What kind of friends are you?" he yelled at us. "Taking sides with a total stranger. You don't deserve to use the name!" Ginger was there, too, standing beside *me*. "It's in the cards," she kept muttering over and over again.

But when I woke up the next morning, I was determined to straighten things out. I decided I'd have a heart-to-heart talk with Kate and Stephanie, and smooth things over. Maybe Patti could help me. She's an excellent peacemaker.

But Patti and Ginger were still fast asleep. Ginger's mouth was open and she was breathing softly. So I slipped out of my room and sneaked down the hall to the spare bedroom.

Kate was already gone! "She's driving to the airport with her dad to pick up her great-aunt Sally for the weekend," Stephanie reminded me. "Remember?"

Stephanie was dressed herself. "I've got to go, too," she said, stuffing her nightshirt and her toothbrush into her tote bag. "Mom, Dad, and I are taking the twins to the city to visit Nana." Nana is Stephanie's grandmother.

"Stephanie, is everything okay?" I said anx-

35

iously. I watched her pull on her sneakers. "With you, Kate, and me, I mean?"

"Sure it is," Stephanie replied briskly. "Why wouldn't it be? See you on Monday morning." She swung her tote bag over her shoulder. "Don't bother to come down. I'll let myself out."

It turned out that Patti couldn't hang around, either. She was going with her parents — they're both college professors — to the university to watch a video documentary about modern-day Eskimos. "Why don't you guys come, too?" she asked Ginger and me.

I love movies about nature and the outdoors, which Eskimos have plenty of. But Ginger shook her head. "Thanks," she said in that slow, husky voice of hers, "but I have an *awful* lot to do today."

So I decided not to go either. I needed some time to myself to think about things, anyway. Maybe Ginger had gotten upset because Kate and Stephanie hadn't paid enough attention to her in the beginning. I remembered how Kate had run in and switched on the TV, and how Stephanie had started moaning about her frizzies. After that, nothing had gone well. . . . Ginger had argued with Kate about movies, which made Kate mad, and then the cards and the Truth or Dare game. . . . Why hadn't I suggested that

36

we all meet at Sun Luck's Chinese Pagoda for dinner first? We might have gotten off to a better start.

Then I thought of what Roger had said when Kate and Stephanie were having problems in the beginning. "They're too much alike — both bossy," and I smiled to myself. Kate and Stephanie had become friends, hadn't they? It had just taken a while. So Kate and Ginger would, too, right? But if I really believed that, why did I have butterflies in my stomach?

Patti left as soon as we'd finished our breakfast. All I could force down was half a bran muffin. I almost never lose my appetite. This Kate versus Ginger business really had me upset.

"I guess your uncle will be picking you up soon," I said to Ginger as we loaded the dishwasher.

"No." She grinned at me. "I didn't want to hurt Patti's feelings, but that Eskimo movie sounded so boring. I'm absolutely free until the moving van gets here, which won't be until late this afternoon."

"Oh." Although I wasn't feeling very cheerful myself, I tried to think of something that would be fun for Ginger. After all, it wasn't her fault everything had gone wrong, was it? "Want to go to the mall?" I suggested. "I'll show you all our favorite places."

"I'd love to!" Ginger said.

Since the weather was a little better, I borrowed Roger's old bike. Ginger used mine, and we rode to the mall.

Our first stop was Sweet Stuff — the best candy store in Riverhurst. I bought some chocolate-covered almonds for later. Then we walked around, peering into windows.

"There's the Pizza Palace," I said, pointing to a small restaurant catty-cornered from Sweet Stuff. "We go there a lot." Pizza Palace is a great place, but it doesn't exactly live up to the second half of its name. In fact, it's about the farthest thing from a palace you could imagine. It's just one small room, crammed with four video games, a long counter, and six stools, with a big black oven against the back wall. Still, their pizza is the best I've ever tasted.

Then we browsed through Romano's, which is this huge store that sells absolutely everything from lawn chairs and trash cans to toys and makeup. Ginger bought some Flash-Pink nail polish, and I picked up the latest issue of *Star Turns*. It had a picture of Kevin DeSpain and Marcy Monroe on the front. Ginger said she couldn't wait to read it.

Next we dropped by the Record Emporium and locked ourselves into a booth to listen to a few cuts from Heat's new album. Heat's my favorite rock group. Ginger said it was hers, too.

We seemed to have everything in common. It was almost weird! But I found myself missing Kate and Stephanie. I really hoped we could work things out *soon*.

Since Mom had given me money for lunch for both of us, Ginger and I decided to eat at Burger Joint. We ordered two cheeseburgers deluxe, a large basket of fries, and two chocolate shakes.

That's when Ginger brought up the subject that had been nagging at me all morning.

"Kate doesn't like me," Ginger said. She dipped a French fry in ketchup. "And Stephanie's not crazy about me, either," she added after she'd popped the fry in her mouth.

I thought there was an excellent chance that Ginger was right, but I didn't want to tell *her* that. "They don't even know you yet!" I argued. "Anyway, Patti likes you."

"Patti's nice," Ginger said. "I'll bet she likes everybody."

I couldn't deny it. Patti does get along with practically everyone.

"It's Kate and Stephanie I'm worried about. You

know what I think? I think they're jealous!"

"Kate and Stephanie?" I said. "Jealous of what?"

"Kate and Stephanie are so used to having you all to themselves, they can't stand it if you make a new friend on your own," Ginger said bluntly.

I shook my head. But inside I wasn't so sure. Maybe Ginger was right! I think Kate *was* a little jealous of my friendship with Stephanie when I'd first introduced them. As soon as *they'd* gotten to be friends, of course, the jealousy went away. Given some time, the same thing would happen with Ginger, wouldn't it?

I hadn't been feeling much like eating all day, but the thought of the five of us as one big, happy group — or at least on speaking terms — cheered me up so much that I gobbled down my burger and fries and drank every drop of my chocolate shake!

After lunch Ginger and I checked out the kittens in Pets of Distinction. There were three tabbies and a calico. They were all six weeks old and totally adorable! Then we walked on up the main aisle of the mall, until we ended up at Just Juniors.

Just Juniors sells terrific clothes for girls. Along with Dandelion on Main Street, it's where the Sleepover Friends most like to shop. And that day the embroidered denim jacket that Patti, Stephanie, and I had been talking about the night before was displayed right in the center of the front window.

The jacket wasn't just embroidered, actually. It was a lot more like a collage. There was lace running along the middle seam in the back, and across the shoulders there was a panel of brown-and-gold velvet flowers. Under it was this big, red-satin rose outlined with rhinestone drops. There were also silver star patches on the sleeves and gold studs on the cuffs. It was incredibly fabulous! A sign underneath it read, "For the student (girl) who sells the most tickets to the Riverhurst Elementary School Art Raffle."

"Wow!" Ginger gasped. "I've never seen a jacket like that!"

"And somebody had to sew all of that stuff on by hand," I said. "It must have taken forever." I could just see myself wearing it to school over my blue high-waisted pants. "It's got to be one of a kind," I added.

The words were barely out of my mouth when Christy Soames came waltzing out of Just Juniors *with the same jacket on*! Actually, it wasn't *exactly* the same as the one in the window — Christy's had large, rhinestone-covered buttons running down the

41

sleeves, instead of star patches, and it had a red fringe along the yoke in the front. But it was close enough.

"Oh, hi, Lauren," Christy said in a bored voice. I'm not trendy enough for Christy to take much interest in me. She turned slowly around to close the door behind her, giving us the full effect of this latest addition to her wardrobe. "How do you like my new jacket?"

"It looks great, Christy," I replied glumly.

Christy *always* looks great. She's probably the best-dressed kid at school. She tells everybody she's going to be a fashion model when she grows up. I guess she could be. She has this sort of golden-brown hair, olive skin, wide blue eyes, and she's tall and thin without being bony. The only problem is every time she opens her mouth she brags about how much her outfits cost, or how she only wears jeans by Gerard St. Vincent, imported from France, or how she couldn't bear to get her hair cut anywhere else but the most expensive salon in the city. She just can't talk about anything but clothes.

Of course, Ginger didn't know all this about Christy, and I could tell she was impressed by what she saw. Ginger nudged me to introduce her.

"Oh. Christy, this is Ginger Kinkaid," I mut-

tered. "She just moved to Riverhurst. Ginger —
Christy Soames."

"Hi!" Ginger said brightly.

Christy's gaze swept Ginger up and down before
she managed a "hi" in return. Then she flicked the
bottom of her hair over her shoulder. The top was
gathered into a loose knot, which would have looked
dorky on almost anyone else, but not on Christy.
"See you around," she said. Then she smiled a self-
satisfied smile and sashayed up on the main aisle.

"Is that the girl who lives on Deerfield?" Ginger
asked, watching Christy veer toward a store called
Dancing Feet. The overhead lights winked off the
rhinestones on Christy's jacket as she bent down to
study the shoes in the window.

I nodded, wondering how many more neat
things Christy was going to snap up that day. Her
parents let her buy practically anything she wants.
"Yeah," I said.

"She's very pretty," Ginger said.

I remembered one of my Grandmother Hunter's
favorite sayings: "Pretty is as pretty does." But I kept
it to myself, because Grandmother Hunter's other
favorite saying is: "If you can't say something nice,
don't say anything!" Instead, I opened the door to

Just Juniors, and Ginger and I stepped inside.

It's always fun to try on clothes, and it's even more fun when you know you might actually buy something. I was definitely in the mood for some serious shopping. Luckily, I had twenty-five dollars to spend, sent by Aunt Beth in her last letter.

There were no embroidered jackets left in Just Juniors, aside from the one in the window. But Ginger and I spent at least an hour trying on mini skirts, stretch pants, overalls, and sweatshirts. By the time we were done I think we'd tried on everything they had on the shelves and racks in our size. I finally picked out a cardigan that was on sale. It was blue with red and turquoise triangles on it. I thought it was really neat-looking.

"We really *do* have the same taste, Lauren," Ginger said approvingly. And she promptly bought the exact same cardigan in green, with yellow and white triangles. I was flattered — it's nice when somebody agrees with your taste enough to spend money on it . . . isn't it?

We paid up, hooked the shopping bags on our handlebars, and rode back to my house. As soon as we got there we put the sweaters on again and grinned at each other in the mirror.

Then I frowned, and tugged at the front of my

44

hair, which was hanging in my eyes, as usual. "I've set it and permed it and moussed it and gelled it," I moaned. "Maybe a crew cut is the only thing left."

"I think your hair would look great in coils," Ginger said. "It's plenty long enough, too. Want to give it a try?"

Ginger showed me how to twist my hair away from my face just like she did hers, starting at the part. "You pin it down every inch or so," she instructed. "See if your mom has any hairpins to hold it with. And it works even better if you twist it while it's wet." Then Ginger started coiling my hair up and tucking the ends under. "You get the idea?"

Did I get the idea! Had someone finally found a way I could beat the stragglies?

After that we read the article about Kevin DeSpain and Marcy Monroe in *Star Turns* together and watched Video Trax for a while on TV. Ginger seemed to like exactly the same groups that I did.

Mr. Blaney honked for Ginger around four. After she'd gone, I practiced on my hair until almost dinnertime. It was starting to look *right*, and more and more like Ginger's.

Ginger had invited me to her house on Sunday, to meet her parents and her two older brothers. But Mom and Dad and I already had plans to drive to

Starkington for the day, to watch my brother, Roger, run in a marathon. Since Starkington's about an hour away from Riverhurst, I didn't see Ginger again until Monday morning, on the steps of Riverhurst Elementary.

Chapter
5

Kate, Stephanie, Patti, and I always meet on the corner of Hillcrest and Pine Street to bike to school together. When I rode up to the corner on Monday morning, Kate and Stephanie were already deep in conversation. But Kate shook her head as soon as she spotted me, and the two of them clammed right up.

"Hi, Lauren!" Stephanie called out cheerily. "Great cardigan!" I was wearing my new sweater, the one I'd bought at Just Juniors.

But Kate's eyes, and Stephanie's, too, were focused on my hair. I'd parted it in the middle and twisted both sides back in neat little coils, just like Ginger had taught me to. I couldn't have been happier with the results. For practically the first time in my life, I didn't feel like a sheepdog, looking at the world from behind a curtain of straggly brown hair.

But neither Stephanie nor Kate could manage to say anything nice about my new hair-do. In fact, they didn't say anything about it, period, although they certainly stared at it enough. It was Patti who exclaimed as she braked to a stop beside us, "Lauren! Your hair looks terrific!"

Right at that moment, Kate and Stephanie both rolled their bikes forward and started coasting down Hillcrest. They also started talking at the same time about what great weekends they'd had.

"I even managed to sell ten more raffle tickets!" Stephanie said as we pedaled toward the school. "Nana bought four, Mrs. Millan across the hall in her apartment building bought two, my friend Kim Bass bought one. Willie the day doorman in Nana's building bought two, and Carl the night doorman, one. The way things are going, the jacket's a cinch to be ours!"

I wondered what Stephanie would say if she knew Christy Soames already *owned* one! But I didn't want to bring up anything about Ginger and me being at the mall together, so I kept my mouth shut.

I'd really hoped Kate and Stephanie would have cooled off about Ginger since Saturday morning, but the signs definitely weren't good. There was the way they were acting about my hair for starters, and the fact that neither of them mentioned the sleepover at my house. But any last hope I had that things would calm down in a hurry died when we reached school. We'd just locked our bikes in the rack in front of Riverhurst Elementary, when I saw Ginger Kinkaid waiting on the front steps, peering at the crowds of kids on the lawn and sidewalk. Her reddish-brown hair was parted in the middle and rolled back on the sides, just like mine was. And she was wearing *her* new cardigan, too!

"What's going on, Lauren?" Kate asked. She looked surprised and kind of hurt. "Were you two twins, separated at birth? The next thing I know, you'll have a Southern accent."

Now Ginger was edging her way down the sidewalk in our direction. "Lauren," she called out over the early-morning dull roar made by hundreds of kids. "Would you mind showing me where Mrs. Wainright's office is? I'm supposed to report there to register, and find out whose class I'm in."

"*Anybody* in Riverhurst could tell her where Mrs. Wainright's office is," Kate whispered snippily to Stephanie.

"And good morning to you, too," I heard Stephanie murmur as Ginger grabbed my sleeve without a word to Stephanie or Kate.

Mrs. Wainwright is the principal at Riverhurst Elementary. I know her office really well, first of all because it's just across the hall from the cafeteria, where I've eaten all my lunches since kindergarten. And second, because I've spent a gruesome couple of hours in there for being late to school.

My general policy is to stay as far away from Mrs. Wainright as possible, but since Ginger needed my help I had to make an exception. We walked through the wide front doors of the school and made a left turn into Mrs. Jamison's cubicle. Mrs. Jamison's the school secretary and a thoroughly nice person. You have to pass through her space to get to Mrs. Wainwright's office.

"Hello, Lauren!" Mrs. Jamison beamed at Ginger and me from behind her desk. "I don't believe I know this young lady. Are you two related?"

The matching hair and cardigans again! "No, Mrs. Jamison," I said. "This is Ginger Kinkaid. She's a new student, and she's supposed to register this morning."

I heard the first bell ring, which means it's time to go to your room. All the kids who'd been hanging around on the lawn poured into the building, jamming the hall outside the office.

"Oh, yes," Mrs. Jamison said. "Now I remember. Mr. Blaney called us about you last week, Ginger."

"I have my report cards from my last school with me," Ginger replied, handing over a big yellow envelope.

"And we've already started a file for you." Mrs. Jamison swiveled around in her chair to pull open a drawer in the file cabinet behind her. She took out a sheet of paper and started asking Ginger a long list of questions, like where she was born and how many schools she had attended.

There's ten minutes from the time the first bell rings until the second bell, which is when you're definitely considered late. The hall was clearing out quickly. I half watched the clock over the file cabinet and half watched the back wall where Mrs. Wainwright's closed office door was. Mrs. Jamison was still writing down the names of all Ginger's old schools, and where they were, and how long she'd gone to each one when Mrs. Wainwright's door slowly swung open.

Mrs. Wainwright is a small woman with silvery

gray hair and pale blue eyes. Henry Larkin says she has a gaze that can turn you to stone. Although, now that I think of it, if she could, Henry would definitely be a statue by now, because he's probably spent more time with Mrs. Wainwright than anybody else in the history of Riverhurst Elementary! Henry's always getting in trouble for goofing off.

But that morning Mrs. Wainwright only smiled pleasantly at Ginger and me and said, "What nice outfits, girls. Are you working on a skit for Mr. Coulter?"

This dressing alike was beginning to get a little embarrassing! Mr. Coulter's the music teacher, and he's also in charge of school talent shows. Even though I liked Ginger, I wasn't sure I wanted to look like her twin sister.

Mrs. Wainwright glanced at the clock and said, "You'd better get to class, Lauren. You're going to be late." I didn't need a second warning. "Good luck!" I mouthed to Ginger. Then I was out of there. I was only sorry I hadn't found out whose class Ginger would be in first.

A few seconds before the late bell rang, I slid into my seat. Kate sits next to me in the second row. She raised an eyebrow at me, and flipped open her math notebook.

"Erin, would you please go to the board and do homework problems one, two, and three?" Mrs. Mead said. "Larry, you may do four through six." Class had begun.

When Ginger didn't show up in our room by the end of math class, I knew she wasn't in 5B with the four of us. It was kind of a relief. I didn't know if I could stand much more strain over Ginger Kinkaid. As it was, even Kate pulled herself together. In the middle of Social Studies she passed me a note: "Lauren, it takes some getting used to, but I'm starting to like your hair. Actually, it looks *good*."

And by the time we trooped down to the basement to the old art studio for our Monday morning art class with Ms. Gilberto, things were almost back to normal.

Ms. Gilberto's kind of a timid person, who doesn't know quite what to do when kids act up. That day, though, Ms. G. was absolutely bubbling! "Not much longer, girls and boys," she said excitedly, "before we'll be out of the basement and into the light!"

Ms. Gilberto meant that the new art studio they were building on the other side of the gym was just about finished. It's above ground, with huge windows and skylights and lots of space. "The outer walls have already been painted white," she told us as we sat down at the long tables. "And now we're ready for our muralists to begin their work!"

The best students from each of the art classes at Riverhurst Elementary would be adding their part to a mural about our school. The mural would stretch around the new studio on three sides. "As you know," Ms. G. added, "the muralists from this class are Sally Mason, Steven Gitten, and Stephanie Green" — Stephanie's especially good at doing people. "And Kate Beekman will videotape them in action." Kate's the vice-president of the Video Club, which Ms. Gilberto sponsors.

"Before I get them set up, though," Ms. Gilberto went on, "how are your raffle-ticket sales going?"

Stephanie's hand shot up. "I need more tickets, Ms. Gilberto," she said. "At least eight . . . no, maybe ten more." She handed over the ticket stubs and the twenty dollars from the last bunch she'd sold.

"Good for you, Stephanie!" Ms. Gilberto said. She handed Stephanie another batch of little red tickets. "Anyone else?"

Pete Stone and Mark Freedman had run out of tickets. Jane Sykes and Karla Stamos had sold all theirs, as well. I'd sold my first ten right away, but I was still working on my second, and so were Kate and Patti.

"Keep it up, class!" Ms. Gilberto said encouragingly after she'd passed out more tickets to all the kids who asked for them. "Now, let's get the rest of you started on this week's project. I'd like you to make a clay mask of any person you really admire. It can be someone living or dead. Someone famous or someone you know well. . . ."

Then Ms. Gilberto pointed to the shelves at the back of the room. "Earlier this morning, 5C, Mr. Patterson's class, modeled everyone from a rock star to Abraham Lincoln to 'just plain folks'," Ms. Gilberto went on. "If you'd like to see who they came up with, take a look at the lower shelf. Single file, please."

We got into line and filed past 5C's shelf one at a time. Kate and Stephanie were ahead of me and Patti was behind me. I could pick out Honest Abe from halfway across the room because of his beard. Chaz from Heat was easy, too, because someone had carefully shaped the snake earring he always wears in his left ear out of a tiny roll of clay.

We'd almost reached the end of the shelf when Stephanie suddenly lurched to a stop. "I can't believe it!" she gasped. "Isn't that *Lauren*?!"

Ms. Gilberto overheard her. "You're absolutely right!" she replied gaily. "A new student named . . . um . . ."

Uh-oh — here it comes. . . , I thought.

"Ginger Kinkaid?" Kate prompted her, with a loud sigh.

"That's it!" Ms. Gilberto said. "Quite talented!"

The brown clay mask had my nose, kind of pinched in the middle and turned up a little at the tip; my eyebrows — thick, straight lines; my mouth, tilted up at the right corner. And my hair — and Ginger's — in coils at the sides!

Kate and Stephanie glanced at each other and shook their heads.

Then Mark Freedman, who was behind Patti in line, said in a loud voice: "Abraham Lincoln meets *Lauren Hunter*?!"

I turned bright red. My face was right next to Honest Abe's, and my head was bigger than his was!

Chapter
6

Maybe I was bigger than Abe Lincoln in some people's eyes, but I was still seriously worried about how to handle lunch. It comes right after art class on Mondays. Kate, Stephanie, Patti, and I always sit together. I was pretty sure that Ginger would want to sit with me, too. And I also had a strong feeling that Kate and Stephanie wouldn't want to sit with Ginger. Ginger wouldn't want to sit with them, either. I didn't know what to do, and just thinking about it was ruining my appetite *again*.

As it turned out I got lucky that day. The muralists and Kate worked straight through lunch period — Ms. Gilberto took them sandwiches from the cafeteria. So only Patti and I were sitting at our usual table when Ginger walked up with her tray.

57

"I got Mr. Patterson!" she announced excitedly, sliding into an empty chair across from me. "He's the best. He cracks jokes all the time and kids around with everybody. . . ."

"You're lucky," Patti said. "Mrs. Milton, in 5A, is really strict."

"And our teacher, Mrs. Mead, gives lots more homework," I told her.

"There are some cute boys in the class, too," Ginger went on, mushing up her mashed potatoes with her fork. We were having meat loaf, mashed potatoes, and gravy that day. "There's one named Tommy something. . . ."

"Brown. Tommy Brown," I said. "He's a terrific baseball player."

"Yech!" Ginger said, scrunching up her nose. "Baseball is so boring."

Well, no one can agree about everything. But then I had a funny thought: What would Ginger say if I told her I loved baseball? Would she say she loved it, too?

"And there's a boy named Bobby," Ginger went on. "With red hair?"

Patti nodded. "Bobby Krieger."

"He's a friend of Kate's," I said. Actually, Kate had liked Bobby at the beginning of the year. I wondered if maybe she had started liking him again, now that she wasn't interested in Royce any more. . . .

"Where *are* Kate and Stephanie?" Ginger asked casually, glancing around the cafeteria.

"Stephanie's working on the mural at the new art studio with some of the other kids," Patti said. "And Kate's videotaping them."

"Oh, yeah. I think a girl in 5C named Betsy is working on it, too," Ginger said.

"We . . . uh . . . saw your mask this morning," I said. I felt kind of uncomfortable about it. I mean, did Ginger know me well enough yet to "really admire" me?

"You did?" Ginger said with a big smile. "What did you think?"

"You're awfully good," Patti said. I guess she'd decided to focus on Ginger's talent, instead of on her choice of subject.

"Thanks. I did lots of clay sculptures at my last school," Ginger said, cutting her meat loaf into little squares before she looked at me. "You liked it, didn't you, Lauren?"

"Yes," I fumbled guiltily. "Yes. I thought it was . . . was nice."

Ginger nodded, satisfied. "Ms. Gilberto gave me a handful of raffle tickets, too," she continued. "But

I don't think I'll have much luck selling them. I mean, I don't *know* anybody here except my family, and I'm getting such a late start."

"There are a few people in my neighborhood that I've missed so far. You could try them, Ginger," Patti said generously.

"I haven't been able to catch the Norrises in, either," I said. "I'll show you their house. It's at the Hillcrest end of my street."

"Thanks, you guys," Ginger said. "Lauren, what about this afternoon? I'll go home and get my bike. . . ."

"I can't today," I said. "I told my mom I'd vacuum the living room and do some washing." Mom has gone back to work full-time, and I help her out by doing chores around the house. Anyway, I felt I could really use a break from *everybody*. "How about tomorrow afternoon?"

"Fine," Ginger agreed. "Today I'll corner my parents and my brothers. They should be good for three or four tickets, at least."

"Hey, Lauren, who's your twin?" Pete Stone flopped down on the chair next to mine and grinned at Ginger across the table.

I could feel my cheeks turning bright red. That does it! I promised myself. I'm never wearing this cardigan to school again. But out loud I only said, "This is Ginger Kinkaid. Ginger, this is Pete Stone."

Pete has wavy, dark brown hair and blue-green eyes, and he's taller than I am. He was wearing his faded denim jacket with the eagle on the sleeve, and even I had to admit he looked pretty good.

Ginger obviously thought so, too. "Hi, Pete," she said. Suddenly her accent, which had almost faded away since Friday, came back stronger than ever. What she said sounded a lot more like, "Hah, Peeete," and she said it really slowly.

"New girl, new girl!" Mark Freedman sang out. "Where are you from?" he asked Ginger as he slid onto the chair beside her.

"Most recently, from Nawth Carolina," Ginger drawled. Her accent was growing with every word!

There was one empty chair left at our table, but not for long. "What are you bothering with these jerks for?" Larry Jackson said, dropping onto it with a thud. "I'm the one who can tell you anything you need to know about Riverhurst Elementary."

"You can?" Ginger giggled.

"You bet!" Larry said. Pete and Mark pulled their chairs in closer. They were all acting like they'd never seen a girl before. Boys can be so aggravating!

"I've got to go, Ginger," I said, picking up my

tray. I really wanted to take my cardigan off and hide it in my backpack before afternoon classes started. "Are you coming?"

Patti stood up, but Ginger stayed put. "See you lay-tuh," she said, waving her fingers at us.

After Patti and I'd dumped our trays, I looked back at the table. Christy Soames was leaning against it, talking to Pete and Mark. I remembered that Christy's in Mr. Patterson's class, same as Ginger.

Of course, my missing cardigan was the first thing Kate picked up on when we came back to 5B after lunch. "No more matchies?" she murmured after the late bell rang.

"Just what do you have against Ginger Kinkaid, anyway?" I whispered huffily.

"I think she's a total phony," Kate said. Stephanie nodded in agreement from her seat in the front row — she was listening to us over her shoulder.

You're both just jealous! is what I was thinking to myself, but what I said was, "You mean her accent? So what?!"

"No, not her *accent*!" Kate muttered.

We didn't have a chance to say anything else, because right about then Mrs. Mead spoke up.

"Quiet, please, class," she said, with a glance

in our direction. "Take out your pencils and get ready for your science quiz."

At the end of the day, though, Kate took up just where we'd left off. "Just what do you *like* about Ginger?" she asked me. She, Patti, Stephanie, and I were hurrying out of the building, toward the bike rack outside. "Besides the fact that she thinks you're as much of a star as Abraham Lincoln."

Stephanie giggled at that. Even Patti smiled a little.

"We happen to have a lot in common!" I replied. I didn't say it, but I was thinking about how Kate wouldn't understand how nice that can be, since she and I have hardly *anything* in common.

"Yeah?" Kate said. "Like what? Your sweaters?"

"Plenty of things!" I said. "Like the same taste in movies and the same favorite color, and . . ."

But Stephanie interrupted me. "Blue's Ginger's favorite color? I don't believe it! Have you ever seen Ginger Kinkaid wearing *blue*?"

Now that she mentioned it, *I* hadn't. Even Ginger's jeans weren't blue — they were black!

"Lauren!" Ginger was yelling at me from down the sidewalk near the curb. She was standing beside a bright blue station wagon. "Come meet my mom!"

63

"Her car is blue!" I said triumphantly. Why were they giving me such a hard time?! And then I went too far and said what I'd been thinking: "You guys are just jealous that Ginger and I are friends!"

Stephanie started to say something, but she snapped her mouth shut. Patti stared down at her feet. Then Kate's face turned beet-red, and it wasn't from embarrassment. "For your information, Lauren Hunter — "

"Lau-ren!" Ginger called again, and I whirled around and marched toward the blue car.

Chapter
7

As it turned out, the car Ginger was standing next to actually belonged to Mrs. Soames. Mrs. Kinkaid's car was being worked on at Vinnie's Auto Repair, and since the Soameses are the Kinkaids' neighbors on Deerfield Lane, Mrs. Soames had given Ginger's mother a ride to Riverhurst Elementary. But Kate and Stephanie and Patti had pedaled away too soon to figure that out.

Mrs. Kinkaid was a big woman, with Ginger's husky voice and her reddish-brown hair. "I really appreciate how nice you've been to Ginger," she told me. "We'd love to have you to dinner, Lauren. What about tomorrow evening?"

"We can sell some of my raffle tickets first!" Ginger said.

"I'll have to ask my mother," I said. "But it sounds fine."

As I rode home alone, I remembered the dream I'd had, with Kate and Stephanie kicking Patti and me out of the Sleepover Friends. In real life, I didn't even have Patti for company! All I had to look forward to was dinner with Ginger Kinkaid. Ginger was okay, but it wasn't the same as an old friend. Maybe her room was blue. . . .

But I never even made it to the Kinkaids' on Tuesday, because late Monday afternoon, when I was jogging with Roger (we run together three or four times a week), I had an accident.

I guess I was still worrying about everything that had been happening instead of paying attention to what I was doing. Anyway, we were coming around the curve at the end of Clearview Crescent, one street over from Pine Street, when it happened.

I must have stepped on a pebble, or a loose piece of paving. All I know is one second I was jogging along with Roger, and the next I was sprawled on the pavement with two scraped knees and a dull ache in my left ankle. By the time Roger kneeled down to look at it, the ankle was already puffing up, and I knew I had a problem.

"I'd better get you home fast, kid," Roger said. "Ice first and then heat."

Roger lifted me up in both arms and carried me through the McBrides' yard to our alley. My ankle really began to throb as we bumped up the back steps.

My mom was in the kitchen, starting dinner. She took one look at my ankle, turned off the oven, loaded me into her car, and drove me straight to the emergency room at Central County Hospital.

We waited for what seemed like hours, but was probably really only twenty minutes or so. Around me people got treated for broken arms, earaches, even dog bites. Meanwhile, my ankle blew up like a blue-and-purple balloon. When it was our turn, a nurse took X rays of the bones in my foot, to see if I'd chipped or broken anything. Mom and I waited again, and finally Doctor Winter called us into her office to tell us that I just had a bad sprain.

"You'll have to stay off it for a couple of days, at least," she said. She wrapped my ankle tightly with an elastic bandage. "Be sure to use a cold pack, Lauren. It will speed the recovery. I'll check you again on Wednesday afternoon. Then you'll be on crutches for a week or so."

Any other time, I probably would have liked the idea of taking a couple of days off from school and lying around and watching TV. But not that week. How would I ever straighten things out with Kate and Stephanie if I was flat on my back?

It wasn't until Mom and I were in the car again, and I was sort of dozing in the back seat — spraining an ankle really wears you out — that I remembered Ginger's cards. The Four of Spades meant a health problem, all right, only it was one that was a lot more serious than a dentist appointment. Then I thought of something even worse. If Ginger's and my friendship was definitely in the cards, too, where did that leave the Sleepover Friends?

My mom called Mrs. Beekman the next morning, to ask her to let Kate know that I wouldn't be riding my bike to school with them. I hoped Kate would get on the phone, but she didn't. "Shows how much she cares," I muttered to myself. Mom stayed home from work that day to help me out, but even so I was pretty miserable. Most of the day I slept, but I kept having dreams about the Sleepover Friends. None of them were good. . . .

At about three thirty-five our front doorbell rang,

and my spirits rose a little. Maybe that's Kate and Stephanie and Patti! I told myself.

But it wasn't. It was Ginger Kinkaid. I was really disappointed. Sure, I liked Ginger. But Kate and Stephanie and Patti and I had a *history*! They knew everything about me, like how I always order banana smoothies at Charlie's Soda Fountain, and how I always have nightmares after watching scary movies, and all kinds of other stuff. Ginger just wasn't the same.

"I heard about your ankle from Patti," Ginger said as she sat at my desk chair.

At least *Patti* was thinking about me!

"I just wanted to see how you're doing." Ginger was wearing green-and-black checked jeans with black cuffs, and a dark gray top, no blue anywhere. Her hair looked different, too. It was pulled up into a knot on the top of her head.

"Great!" I said gloomily.

Stephanie and Kate would have at least tried to cheer me up, but Ginger didn't seem to notice how down I was feeling. She asked, "Which house is the Norrises', anyway?"

"It's five houses up the street, on the right." I was feeling worse and worse. "It's yellow. If you'll look out the window. . . ."

Ginger opened my bedroom window and leaned out. "Yellow with black shutters?" she asked. "I see it." She glanced down the street. Then she quickly slammed the window shut. "Listen, Lauren, I've got to go. I'm really glad you're okay, though." She grinned at me. "I'll see you tomorrow." I think she was out of my room, down the stairs, and out the front door in about thirty seconds flat. I remembered all the hours Kate spent with me when I had the measles in the second grade. And last year, when Kate and Stephanie took turns bringing me ice cream from Charlie's Soda Fountain for my strep throat.

I was really hoping Patti would call that evening, or possibly even Stephanie, or Kate. But every time the phone rang, it was for Roger.

My appointment with Dr. Winter at the hospital was at three forty-five the next day. So I didn't know if anyone came by my house after school or not. The doctor unwrapped my bandage and felt around on my ankle. The blue and purple was shading into green and lavender by then. It wasn't quite as swollen, either.

The doctor smiled encouragingly and wrapped it neatly back up. "Lauren, I'd like you to stay off your feet one more day," she said. "Then you may go to school if you take it easy."

Another whole day! By then Kate and Stephanie and Patti will have forgotten all about me, I thought glumly, and chosen a replacement!

But Patti called me that night. She said she'd had a meeting of the Quarks Club the afternoon before, so she hadn't been able to stop by. Our phone had been busy all Tuesday evening, she told me. She just couldn't get through. Thanks a million, Roger! I thought. But she made it over the next day.

Patti brought me up to date on what I'd missed in class, but I couldn't help noticing that she didn't say a word about Kate or Stephanie. It made me feel awful. But then I got mad. I was the one with the sprained ankle, and they hadn't come to see me or even called once!

If they didn't want to know about me, I sure wasn't going to ask about them either!

"You'll be at school tomorrow?" Patti asked. I nodded. "Great!" she said. "We're having an assembly in the gym for the raffle, first thing, and then Ms. Gilberto will unveil the murals at the new art studio."

It wasn't until Patti had left and Mom brought in my dinner on a tray that I realized that I hadn't heard from Ginger Kinkaid all afternoon. The Sleepover Friends were going down the tubes, and Ginger wasn't turning out to be such a great friend after all. Dinner was my favorite — steak with mushroom gravy — but I could hardly eat it. I wondered if I'd ever get my appetite back again!

On Friday morning, Mom took me to school late, so I wouldn't get jostled. I'd dressed all in blue — blue overalls, a blue sweater with pale-green stripes, even blue sneakers, and my hair wasn't coiled. I'd just let it hang in my face, the old way.

Mom and I checked into Mrs. Wainwright's office. Then Mom went on to work, and I headed for the gym. Mrs. Jamison went with me, to help out if I needed it. I wasn't exactly an expert at using my crutches. We sat in the last row at the back. I propped my left leg up on a folding chair.

All the kids at Riverhurst Elementary were spread out in front of us, whispering, fidgeting, coughing, and giggling. But they quieted down fast when Mrs. Wainwright stepped onto the stage at the front of the gym.

Mrs. Wainwright made a speech about the new art studio being the realization of all her dreams, and Ms. Gilberto's. While she went on about the years of planning that had gone into it and how much help everyone had been, I tried to pick Kate, Stephanie, and Patti out of the crowd, or even Ginger Kinkaid, for that matter. I thought I spotted Patti's head sticking up above the others about twenty rows in front of me. She's the tallest girl in fifth grade, so she's usually pretty easy to find. But I stopped looking when Mrs. Wainwright said, "Here's Ms. Gilberto for the drawing!"

Ms. Gilberto walked onstage and grabbed the microphone in a death grip. She gets totally freaked out if she has to talk to more than twenty-five people at once. "Good morning, boys and girls," she said in a sort of strangled voice. "First I want to tell you about the raffle-ticket sales. Many of you really outdid yourselves. Martin Yates, in fourth grade, sold thirty-five tickets" — she stopped for applause — "and Ricky Delman, a sixth-grader, sold thirty seven."

I was wondering if that beat Stephanie's total when Ms. Gilberto said in the next breath, "Stephanie Green — " there was a wild burst of applause from the audience. Stephanie actually did it! I thought excitedly. The jacket's *ours*! But then I corrected myself sadly. "Or theirs. . . ." Why would Stephanie and Kate want to share a jacket with someone they couldn't be bothered to even call when she was in bed with a sprained ankle?

"Stephanie Green sold thirty-nine raffle tickets,"

Ms. Gilberto announced, holding up her hands for quiet. "Even more astonishing," she continued, "a brand-new student managed to sell *forty-three tickets* in four days: Ginger Kinkaid!"

Cheers broke out and I heard a long, loud whistle I recognized as Pete Stone's. Was *Ginger* getting the jacket? After all her complaints about not knowing anyone in Riverhurst, and only being able to sell tickets to her family?! Forty-three tickets is a mighty big family!

But no, Ms. Gilberto was still talking. "But our most successful salesperson," Ms. Gilberto squeaked excitedly, "sold a staggering sixty-seven raffle tickets! She" — So it *was* a girl, but who? — "will be awarded the beautiful embroidered denim jacket that has been hanging in the window of Just Juniors all week long." Ms. Gilberto paused again, and beamed at the audience. "And that person is . . . Karla Stamos!"

Karla Stamos! I couldn't believe it. Karla Stamos wearing the most fabulous jacket in the world? It was enough to make you cry, or giggle. Karla practically lives in brown or beige. She's a total grind, too, and she insists on giving everyone study advice, whether you ask for it or not.

On the other hand, I certainly didn't want *Ginger*

to beat Stephanie. I had a feeling that would definitely finish the Sleepover Friends!

"Come on up here, Karla!" Ms. Gilberto motioned her forward. Karla clumped up the steps onto the stage, in her brown corduroys and beige sweater, to accept her gift certificate for the jacket. No one cheered much except for Mrs. Wainwright, who applauded from her folding chair.

Then it was time for the drawing. A sixth-grade boy carried a large wire trash can onto the stage, absolutely crammed with little red ticket stubs. Ms. Gilberto called on a first-grader — one of the Reese twins — to come up and pick the winning ticket. She set the trash can on the floor at the front of the stage, the little Reese boy squeezed his eyes shut, jammed his whole arm into the can, and pulled out the winning stub.

"Thank you, Danny," Ms. Gilberto said. "The winning ticket for the all-expenses-paid trip for two to San Francisco is . . . number four three seven eight — Willie Avila!"

"Willie Avila!" Stephanie shrieked from the audience. "That's Nana's doorman!"

So at least one person we knew and liked was getting something out of a thoroughly dismal situation.

After that Mrs. Wainwright took the microphone again. She announced that the raffle had brought in almost *eight thousand dollars*, and she listed all the art supplies the money would buy, like easels and brushes, a larger pottery kiln, another video camera, and tons of other stuff. Then Mrs. Wainwright said, "Now I'd like everyone to file out of the gym through the side door and walk around to the new studio. Ms. Gilberto will unveil the lovely murals which I'm sure we'll all enjoy."

At last I spotted Kate and Stephanie and Patti, when their row stood up, but they were too busy talking, probably about Karla or Ginger, to see me. They didn't even look in my direction.

Mrs. Jamison and I were still waiting for the gym to clear out when I got my next major shock of the day: *Ginger Kinkaid and Christy Soames were twins!* As they stood together, I spotted not only matching hair-dos — loose buns on the top of their heads, fastened down with matching rhinestone hair-clips — but they were wearing *matching embroidered denim jackets!*

Chapter
8

For a moment I was too stunned to think. Then I started wondering if Kate and Stephanie had been right after all. Maybe Ginger Kinkaid really *was* a phony. She hadn't called or come by since Tuesday. Maybe she'd only been nice to me in the first place because Mr. Blaney had set it up, and she didn't know anybody else. Then she and I turned out to be in different classes. . . . Christy Soames was a snappy dresser, pretty, and she just happened to be in 5C, too. . . . Something told me I should have listened to the tried and true.

I was so upset that I didn't pay any attention to where Mrs. Jamison was guiding me. When I eventually came out of my trance, she'd already set a folding chair down for me. The chair and I were right in the center of a huge half-circle of kids gathered around the new art studio.

Ms. Gilberto gave a short speech. I hardly heard a word of it, because I was too busy thinking what an absolute jerk I'd been. Would Kate and Stephanie ever speak to me again?

Then Ms. Gilberto said, "Now, I'll just pull this cord — " She tugged on a piece of red rope, which was attached to the canvas curtain that was hanging over the murals. Nothing happened. "I'll just pull this cord. . . ," Ms. Gilberto repeated, jerking on the rope with both hands. She was starting to look a little desperate. At last the canvas came tumbling down, the way it was supposed to, uncovering the murals underneath.

The murals were great! They looked like a big patchwork quilt with all these different scenes at Riverhurst Elementary on it. There were pictures of kids on the playground and someone had painted Tommy Brown and Mark Freedman and Bobby Krieger playing baseball with a bunch of other boys. There were scenes in the classrooms, like Mrs. Milton pointing her ruler at Kyle Hubbard and looking stern, and my fourth-grade teacher, Mr. Civello, pretending to scowl at the kids in 4A. His black hair was standing on end, the way it usually does in real life.

There were scenes in the gym of a play-practice, with Mr. Coulter directing, scenes in the library, scenes in the old art studio. And finally there were all these pictures of the cafeteria, with kids sitting at their favorite tables. Pete Stone and Larry Jackson were eating hot dogs. Karla Stamos was reading a book in the corner — they'd have to repaint her with the jacket on now. Six little kids were grouped around their first-grade teacher, and . . . at first I could hardly believe my eyes! It was *us*! Stephanie had painted Kate and herself and Patti and me, sitting together at our regular table. Kate had one blonde eyebrow raised, as usual; Patti was smiling, and Stephanie and I were laughing our heads off!

Stephanie painted us this week, *after* the trouble with Ginger, I was thinking. Which means she still cares a little. . . . I turned around in my chair to look for her.

I finally spotted Stephanie, Kate, and Patti at the back of the half-circle of kids. All three of them were grinning at me, and Kate made the thumbs-up sign! I breathed a sigh of relief so loud that Mrs. Jamison thought I was in pain. But I was so happy I couldn't help myself.

It was the Sleepover Friends forever, for all the world to see, on the outside wall of the new Riverhurst Elementary School art studio!

Our sleepover was at the Greens' that night. It was just as well, because I'm not too swift at going up and down stairs on crutches, and Stephanie's little cottage in the backyard is on just one floor. Mr. Green had it built for her before the twins were born, so she'd have a place to get away from it all.

"Ginger told Kate and me on Tuesday afternoon that you didn't want to see us," Stephanie was explaining to me. "We were just about to head up your walk — "

"You're kidding me!" I said. "She must have seen you from the window of my bedroom!" I was remembering that Ginger had been looking for the Norrises' house when she suddenly decided to leave in a hurry. From my place on Stephanie's couch, I reached for one of Mrs. Green's peanut-butter-chocolate-chip cookies and bit down on it angrily.

"And since she'd just waltzed out your front door, we believed her," Kate said.

"We were pretty upset. . . ." said Stephanie.

"But Ginger never even mentioned your names!" I exclaimed. "And neither did I!"

We hadn't had time to discuss the Ginger Kinkaid mess at school that day. There is *no* privacy in the cafeteria, and Roger had picked me up at three in his car because Mom had insisted I go home and rest before Stephanie's sleepover.

"We should have known it was just one of Shifty's tricks," Kate said, shaking her head.

"Shifty?" I repeated.

Stephanie nodded. "That's what they call her at Camp Minnewaska. My friend Kim Bass goes there. When I was in the city last weekend I asked her all about Ginger."

"She said Ginger's the kind of girl who only has one best friend at a time," Kate said, "and she dumps them as soon as she finds someone. . . ."

"Better?" I finished for her gloomily. I mean, who likes to think of herself as second-rate, especially when the competition is as dopey as Christy Soames?

"Not necessarily," Stephanie said quickly. "Just *different*. Last summer alone, Ginger had four best friends in a row — "

"Short attention span," Kate interrupted.

". . . one at a time, of course, ending up with a girl named Suzy Vandervettering, who Kim said is a snob and a total jerk," Stephanie reported. "I guess Ginger was running out of possibilities."

" 'Shifty' Kinkaid! Why didn't you tell me before?" I groaned. I mean, Ginger was about as dependable as Pete Stone!

"Kate wouldn't let me," Stephanie said.

"I know how stubborn you are, Lauren," Kate said with a grin. "I thought it might make you twice as determined. about Ginger. You had to see for yourself."

"But you thought there was something funny about her right away!" I said.

"I might have been a teeny bit jealous in the very beginning," Kate admitted. "I don't like changes very much . . . as you've probably noticed. But then I spotted something funny about what she did with the cards."

"What about them?" I asked.

"Ginger didn't shuffle them," Stephanie said. "She wanted to be sure they came out in the right order. So that they'd predict she'd be your new best friend."

"And she doesn't like to share a friend with anybody, remember?" said Kate. "She was *trying* to split us up."

"But what about the four of spades and health problems?" I asked, pointing to my bandaged ankle.

"Lau-ren, you can be kind of a klutz when

you've got things on your mind," Kate said. "So you fell down. A coincidence."

I grinned. Kate really does hate mumbo-jumbo.

"But why did Ginger bother to lie to you on Tuesday, if she'd already fastened onto Christy Soames?" I asked.

"She probably wasn't sure it was going to work out yet with Christy," said Kate. "But by Wednesday they were thick as thieves!"

"Well, I know one thing you guys don't know," I said. "I know where Ginger sold those forty-three raffle tickets."

"Where?" Kate, Stephanie, and Patti were all ears.

"Mr. Blaney sold them at the office!" I said. "Dad told me this evening that all the employees bought them."

"I know where Karla sold hers," Patti said then.

"I bet I know, too," Kate interrupted. "At her aunt and uncle's card store on Main Street."

"Right!" Patti said.

"What I want to know is, where did Ginger get that jacket?" I asked. "There weren't any left at Just Juniors."

"I know that, too," Patti replied wisely. "I overheard her talking to Christy about it in the lunch line yesterday. I just didn't realize she intended to *buy* one."

"Well?" Stephanie said. "Out with it. Where did she get it?" She was still a little upset because we hadn't won.

"Dandelion," Patti told us. That's the kids' store on Main. "They had four of them, in four different sizes."

"Twins for life, or until the jackets wear out," Stephanie sniffed.

"But Ginger and Christy aren't just twins anymore — they're triplets," Kate pointed out.

"Who's the third?" we asked.

"Karla Stamos!" Kate said. "Shifty, the Model . . . and Karla Stamos!"

And all four of us burst out laughing!

It was fabulous to be together again! Some people can only manage one best friend, but I got lucky — I have *three!* And something I'll never get tired of . . . Sleepover Friends forever!

#21 Starstruck Stephanie

Stephanie slid into her desk not thirty seconds before the late bell rang! Although Kate and I sit right behind her, she didn't turn around to whisper anything to us.

At lunchtime Stephanie bolted out and raced to the cafeteria. But Kate, Patti, and I were close behind.

"Now we can talk," I said to Stephanie. "So come on . . . . What was your dad's big surprise?"

"Well . . ." Stephanie said. 'I had no idea where Dad wanted to take me, right?" She paused. Stephanie usually loves surprises, but she didn't seem to be enjoying this one very much.

"Stephanie! Was yesterday fabulous or what?" someone screeched practically in my ear.

It was the dreaded Jenny Carlin!

"Kevin was even better-looking than he is on TV, didn't you think?" Jenny shrieked even louder.

"Better-looking than he is on TV!" Kate said in a stern voice. "That was your surprise? You saw Kevin DeSpain *in person*, Stephanie?!

Patti and I stared at Stephanie, absolutely speechless.

WIN GIRL TALK DATE LINE –
AN AUDIO DATING GAME!

Enter the
SLEEPOVER™
FRIENDS
Date Line Giveaway!

100 Winners!

It's new! It's exciting! And you can win one! It's GIRL TALK DATE LINE ™ — the game of make-believe and fun! Play it at your next sleepover! Listen to the recorded phone calls and match up boys and girls for dates! Just fill in the coupon below and return by March 1, 1990.

Rules: Entries must be postmarked by March 1, 1990. Winners will be picked at random and notified by mail. No purchase necessary. Valid only in the U.S.A. Void where prohibited. Taxes on prizes are the responsibility of the winners and their families. Employees of Scholastic Inc.; its agencies, affiliates, subsidiaries; and their immediate families not eligible. For a complete list of winners, send a stamped, self-addressed envelope to Sleepover Friends Date Line Giveaway, Contest Winners List, at the address provided below.

Fill in the coupon below or write the information on a 3" x 5" piece of paper and mail to:
SLEEPOVER FRIENDS DATE LINE GIVEAWAY,
Scholastic Inc., P.O. Box 673, Cooper Station, New York, NY 10276.

SLEEPOVER FRIENDS Date Line Giveaway

Name _____ Age _____

Street _____

City _____ State _____ Zip ____

Where did you buy this Sleepover Friends book?
☐ Bookstore ☐ Drug Store ☐ Supermarket ☐ Discount Store
☐ Book Club ☐ Book Fair ☐ Other (specify) _____

SLE689

America's Favorite Series

THE BABY-SITTERS CLUB®

Collect Them All!

by Ann M. Martin

The seven girls at Stoneybrook Middle School get into all kinds of adventures...with school, boys, and, of course, baby-sitting!

☐ MG41588-3	**Baby-sitters on Board! Super Special #1**	**$2.95**
☐ MG41583-2	**#19 Claudia and the Bad Joke**	**$2.75**
☐ MG42004-6	**#20 Kristy and the Walking Disaster**	**$2.75**
☐ MG42005-4	**#21 Mallory and the Trouble with Twins**	**$2.75**
☐ MG42006-2	**#22 Jessi Ramsey, Pet-sitter**	**$2.75**
☐ MG42007-0	**#23 Dawn on the Coast**	**$2.75**
☐ MG42002-X	**#24 Kristy and the Mother's Day Surprise**	**$2.75**
☐ MG42003-8	**#25 Mary Anne and the Search for Tigger**	**$2.75**
☐ MG42419-X	**Baby-sitters' Summer Vacation Super Special #2**	**$2.95**
☐ MG42503-X	**#26 Claudia and the Sad Good-bye**	**$2.95**
☐ MG42502-1	**#27 Jessi and the Superbrat**	**$2.95**
☐ MG42501-3	**#28 Welcome Back, Stacey!**	**$2.95**
☐ MG42500-5	**#29 Mallory and the Mystery Diary**	**$2.95**
☐ MG42499-8	**Baby-sitters' Winter Vacation Super Special #3**	**$2.95**
☐ MG42498-X	**#30 Mary Anne and the Great Romance**	**$2.95**
☐ MG42497-1	**#31 Dawn's Wicked Stepsister** (February '90)	**$2.95**
☐ MG42496-3	**#32 Kristy and the Secret of Susan** (March '90)	**$2.95**
☐ MG42495-5	**#33 Claudia and the Mystery of Stoneybrook** (April '90)	**$2.95**
☐ MG42494-7	**#34 Mary Anne and Too Many Boys** (May '90)	**$2.95**
☐ MG42508-0	**#35 Stacey and the New Kids on the Block** (June '90)	**$2.95**

For a complete listing of all the Baby-sitter Club titles write to :
Customer Service at the address below.
Available wherever you buy books...or use the coupon below.

Scholastic Inc. P.O. Box 7502, 2932 E. McCarty Street, Jefferson City, MO 65102

Please send me the books I have checked above. I am enclosing $_____

(please add $2.00 to cover shipping and handling). Send check or money order–no cash or C.O.D.'s please.

Name_____

Address_____

City_____ State/Zip_____

Please allow four to six weeks for delivery. Offer good in U.S.A. only. Sorry, mail order not available to residents of Canada.   Prices subject to change.   BSC 789

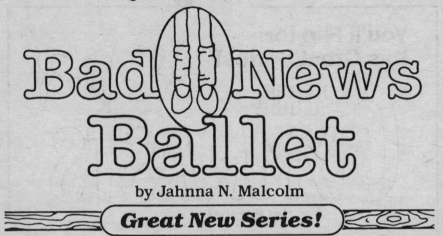